One Smart Fish

Some other books by Chris Wormell:
The Big Ugly Monster and the Little Stone Rabbit
Ferocious Wild Beasts
George and the Dragon
George, the Dragon and the Princess
Henry and the Fox
In the Woods
Molly and the Night Monster
Off to the Fair
The Saddest King
Scruffy Bear and the Six White Mice
The Sea Monster
Two Frogs
The Wild Girl

ONE SMART FISH
A RED FOX BOOK 978 1 862 30652 3

First published in Great Britain by Jonathan Cape,
an imprint of Random House Children's Publishers UK
A Random House Group Company

Jonathan Cape edition published 2010
Red Fox edition published 2011

5 7 9 10 8 6 4

Red Fox Books are published by Random House Children's Publishers UK,
61–63 Uxbridge Road, London W5 5SA

www.**randomhousechildrens**.co.uk
www.**randomhouse**.co.uk

Addresses for companies within The Random House Group Limited can be found at: www.randomhouse.co.uk/offices.htm

THE RANDOM HOUSE GROUP Limited Reg. No. 954009

A CIP catalogue record for this book is available from the British Library.

Printed in China

One Smart Fish

Chris Wormell

Red Fox

Long ago, before you were born, and before I was born, and before anyone in the whole world was born . . . .

the ocean was filled with amazing fish.

(It still is, of course, only they were

more amazing then.)

Some were amazingly colourful, like these.

Some were amazingly weird, like this one.

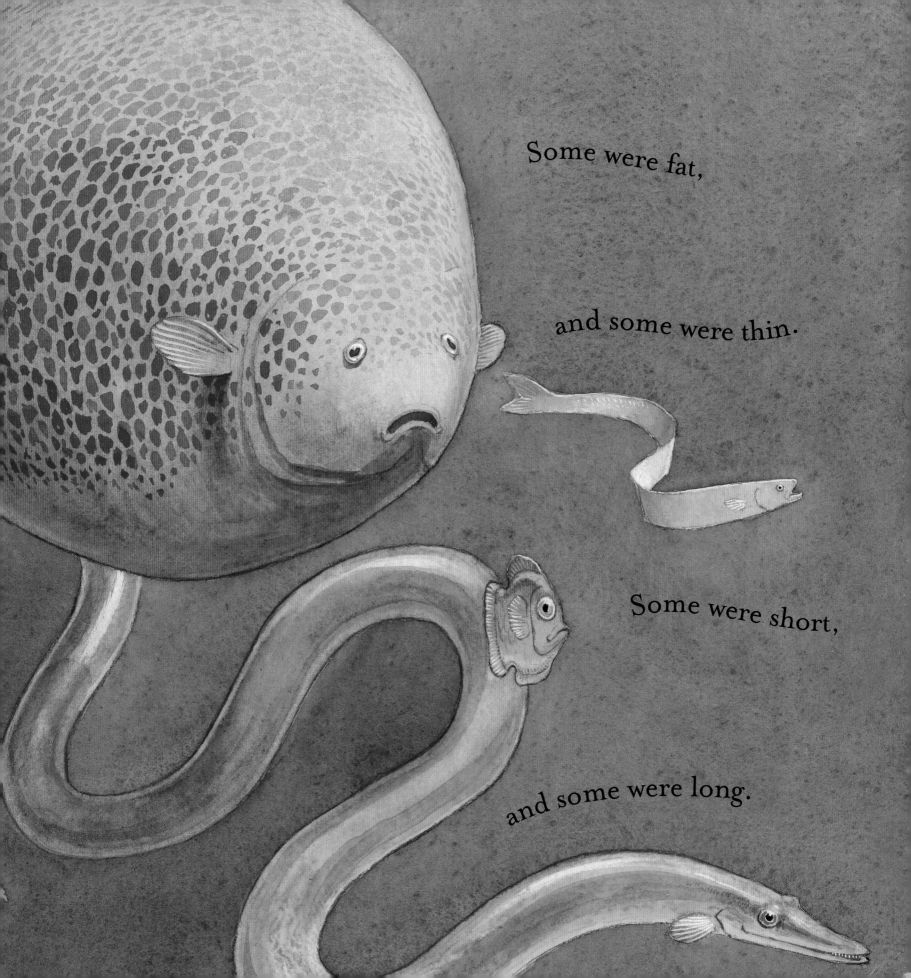

Some were fat,

and some were thin.

Some were short,

and some were long.

Some were big
and some were small.

Some were cute,
and some were . . . .

SCARY!

But the most amazing fish
of all . . .

He was wonderfully smart.

Smarter than **all** the other
fish in the ocean
put together.

He was **SO** smart he could do almost anything.
He could sing and dance and make wonderful music.

He could draw fantastic pictures and perform marvellous plays.
This fish was a genius.

And yet he was not content. For there was one thing he
wanted to do more than anything else, and it was the one thing
he couldn't do – he wanted to walk upon the land.

DANGER
SHALLOW WATER

Every year, when all the fish went up to the
landside for their holidays, the smart fish would
gaze up at the beach, longing to explore the world;
to feel the wind on his face and the sun on his scales.
But everyone knows that fish can't walk . . . can they?

Well, this fish was not going to be put off by a little thing like that.
So he thought long and hard until at last he came up

with a brilliant idea . . .

FEET!

(It sounds obvious now, but back then no one had ever heard of feet.)
So the smart fish made himself a beautiful set of feet
and slipped them on over his fins.

and walked up the beach!

He was the first fish ever,
in the history of the world, to walk upon
the land. And not just the first fish — he was
the first CREATURE ever to walk upon the land.

There was no one else. The place was empty.
(Well, there may have been a few bugs and insects, but that was all.)

The smart fish was bored and lonely.

So he dived back into the ocean to join all the other fish!

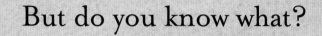

But do you know what?

That walking idea eventually caught on, and a few years later (it may have been a few **million** years later) some other fish tried it. They weren't clever enough to make feet of their own, so they slithered up the beach, crawling on their fins . . .

. . . which is not nearly so good
as walking of course, so after a few years
(it may have been a few **hundred million** years)
they grew feet instead of fins.

And then guess what?

They weren't fish any more — they were reptiles!

Then they really started
changing, and all this
started happening.